good deed rain

Florida © 2019
Allen Frost, Good Deed Rain
Bellingham, Washington
ISBN 978-1-64516-986-4

Writing and Cartoons: Allen Frost
Cover: Hanah Lee
Cover Assistance: Jen Armitage
Apple: TFK!

Some of these stories originally appeared in rare hand-sewn or stapled editions of: *Pie in the Sky, King Leopold's Slow Leak, Royalty Toy Company, Trelawny Cable Car, Sacred Heart Junkyard, A Parents' Guide to Raising Piranhas, The Time Has Come to Make All the Machines Fly, 500 Pound Halo, One Eye Open, Radio, A Reversed Cat, Animals Ghosts & Outer Space, The Peaceful Island, Snow White Moth.*

For Rosa

"It all begins with keeping faith with something that grows and changes as you go on."
—F. Scott Fitzgerald, *Letters to His Daughter*

FLORIDA

34 Books by Allen Frost

....Ohio Trio................Bowl of Water....

....Another Life..............Home Recordings....

.............The Mermaid Translation............

..The Selected Correspondence of Kenneth Patchen..

..The Wonderful Stupid Man........Saint Lemonade..

......Playground.................Roosevelt......

...5 Novels.................The Sylvan Moore Show...

..............Town in a Cloud..............

......A Flutter of Birds Passing Through Heaven:

A Tribute to Robert Sund......

...At the Edge of America.....Lake Erie Submarine...

...The Book of Ticks........I Can Only Imagine...

......The Orphanage of Abandoned Teenagers.....

................Different Planet..............

...Go with the Flow: A Tribute to Clyde Sanborn...

....Homeless Sutra.............The Lake Walker....

.........A Hundred Dreams Ago.........

....Almost Animals.........The Robotic Age....

..........Kennedy.................Fable..........

.......Elbows & Knees: Essays & Plays.......

...............The Last Paper Stars..............

..........Walt Amherst Is Awake..........

......When You Smile You Let in Light......

.....Pinocchio in America.........Florida.....

FLORIDA

ALLEN FROST

Good Deed Rain ◊ Bellingham, Washington ◊ 2019

INTRODUCTION

At the start of March, we took 3 days to visit our daughter who was working at Disneyworld. This collection of travel dispatches resulted from that expedition. Florida was so unlike the winter of Bellingham, it was like being dipped into a surreal cartoon. Feeling that way, I include some drawn stories too. As long as that feeling lasted, this book continued to be broadcast. Thanks to sunshine.

Heaven
the lights
the flowers
the warmth
who could forget
who wouldn't
want to go
back.
3/9/19 Florida

Sun inspired these stories, but once we were back in Washington I noticed Florida begin to fade. It was hard to know exactly when this book would be done, whatever was pushing it along was weather-driven. The cold gray April rain arrived. I stopped in a field on the way home from work and I found the last reminder. A wet map of dandelions spread across the grass like stars. Florida wasn't imaginary, what follows is proof we had been there.

CONTENTS

A Chair for Manatees
The Talking Dog Store
Chocolate Hair
You Are Made of Flowers
Ann Margaret
The Robot
80 Degrees in Winter
Plastic Telephone
Dreams of Making a Living
Florida Lizard
A Wild Goose Chase
Contrails
Lobsters
The Wolf of Cocoa Beach
Tribute to Lord Buckley
Bicycles
The Daily Fly
Morris Teahorn
Remember Abbott & Costello
The 3 Stooges
21 Circus Rooms
And Their Stars
Eddie
A Florida Clown
The Ocelot

A. Robins, The Banana Man
Eddie Bracken
A Starfish
Dr. Biocal's Butterflies
The World's Most Hated Man
The Cloud Driver
The Flying Machine of Mr. Green
A Chair For Manatees: The Movie
The Talking Tiger
Broken Paddle
The Shoe Salesman
Bookies
6 Moths
Garage Sale Joke
The Gardenia
7 Pictures
Son of 6 Moths
Tourist Attraction
The Daily Fly Returns
Tin Moses
Some Other World
On the Trail of the Mummy
In the Footsteps of Zorro
Vic Shingles' Ghastly Puppets
The Compassion I Used to Have is Gone Now

Yor
Old What's-His-Face
Inspector Ozawa
Vic Shingles' Ghastly Puppets Encore
Shark Cage Smith
A Frog
Over Milkweed
Plastic Jobs
A Duck
A Cat
Snow White Moth
The Great Composers
200 Zoos
The Spectacular Failure of Gaston LeFlue, 1891
The Girl Who is the River
Huckleberries
A Silent Movie
New Shoes
A Bat
A Rabbit
The Piano Tuner
The Cobra Handler
A Coyote
Two Crows
That Flower

Crows
Blackberries
Grapefruits
Richard Is Gone
The Reddish Dog
The Dark Boat
The Local Author
The Usual Story
The Dream Factory
Really and Truly
The Old Astronaut
The Sleepy Tiger
Territory
Cape Canaveral
This Is My Bread and Butter
Beethoven Sonata #8 Performed by a Snowman
A Dead Honey Bee
The Palm Reader
Florida Crickets
Spirit Airlines
A Bird
Flying Tangerine
Heaven
31 Swans
Winter Flowers

The Mallards
Singing Sunlight
The Queen of Stripes
Nostalgia City
ICU2TV
The Start of Japan
The Daffodil Gang
Apples
The Cat Who Walked In Cement
A Reversed Man
The World is Cliff Link
Cliff Link Makes a Telephone Call
The Lunatic
A 1973 Dream
A 1944 Movie
The Time Machine Salesman
The Family I Left Behind
5 AM
5:30 AM
6 AM

The Missing Bird

Our house is quiet without her. The corner where she sang is empty air.

Radio Forest

Beginning in Washington and sleeping in the woods, in the cold clean air of fir and cedar, where the trees are tall black radio towers talking to us.

The Airport Rabbit

It was 15 degrees outside, cold enough for winter snow to pile in the grass between the runway
lights. Two white jets are parked and service
trucks come and go. I chose this plastic seat by
the window to watch this unremarkable airport
scene. It could have stayed that way, like the
picture on a china plate, but suddenly something loped into view. A pet rabbit. It took its
time, going under the ramp and out of sight.

Florida Telephone

We've never gone this long without our daughter near. For 3 months we only know her voice in a telephone.

Photograph with Sound of Crows

Across from the IHOP crows in a row of
palm trees.

The Ant

We rented an ant to get around Orlando. That was the only way to navigate all the cement stop and go. Mostly it knew its way around but one time we took the wrong exit off the interstate and we had to turn around in a used car lot.

The rust and wear of the road disappears. That bright color is back. The chrome shines. The wheels just left the factory assembly line and the radio is on.

The Dream Water

Blue Springs runs through this reality. I can't describe the peace and clarity of the water. All I can do is stare. Even the fish can't seem to believe they are here. They tap the surface to test it.

Modern Piano Moving

This is a fairy tale. Three times we left the interstate to pay the toll, then we got stuck behind that slow truck again. Each time I read the slogan I wondered, "What makes piano moving modern?" It's been going on since before Laurel & Hardy. Maybe a clue is its destination. We're on the road to Cape Canaveral. Maybe that white moving truck is headed for a delivery to the moon.

The Sea Monster

It came all the way from Delaware. It's so tired that first morning it leans on the pier.

"Sorry," the tour guide told everyone. "There aren't any pelicans today." They were all inside the beach house, watching TV. Probably a leisurely breakfast too. I should have crossed the sand to look in the window. But we promised we wouldn't bother the stars.

I bought sweet tea for my daughter at the Winn Dixie. The cashier was new. She was in a rising tide of panic. The receipt tape rolled over her arm like a poisonous snake. The other cashier had to run over and help. My daughter has a job like this and I remember being in those shoes. Customers are lining up, machinery in revolt, a million things are going wrong. Out in the rental car, my son and wife are watching the grackles.

The Upside-Down Cloud

Sitting in the blue sky, it just turned over. All the pots and pans rattled down, all the loose change and cushions off chairs. With everything in a jumble, it floats like a whale, silent until it rolls again.

King of the Sand

The vultures haven't got him yet. He was King of the Sand and as long as he stayed there he was fine. Taking the interstate that day was a mistake. A truck was parked off the shoulder in rutted tracks. Someone stood beside the gate, rigging a fishing line. That scene passed and then he saw something move in the leaves. At first he thought it was a giant spider. The backs of ten slate gray vultures hunched around a dead deer.

Burt Ives, the legendary folk singer,
recently became the first musician in space.

120,000 miles from Earth,
cramped into a bullet-shaped capsule,

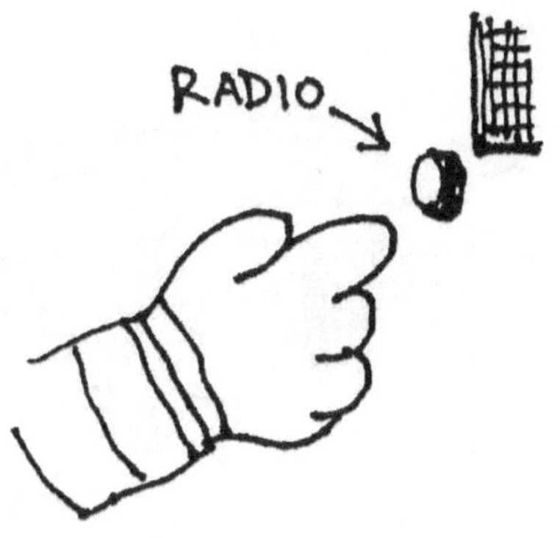

Burt tuned in to Cape Canaveral for a report.

Televisions all over the world showed the scratchy picture of Burt Ives looking pale and terrified.

Someone at Houston Control cut in nervously and asked, "Hey Burt, could you play *My Green Teenybopper?*"

Millions of people watched him hopefully

as he struggled for his guitar under the emergency oxygen supply.

The Happening

The Happening was a long time ago when America allowed itself magic and it wasn't uncommon to turn the corner and see things. A ten foot giant dancing with a painted girl. Kaleidoscope slides projected on the wall. And your father read his poems to another world. Oblivious. His voice tilted. You saw a small blue spider right there on his temple, listening to him.

Water & Air
    For J. Genius

You said, "If I stepped very gingerly, I could walk on water. The surface dipped down a little at each step and had a saran-wrap like quality but would hold me up." I know the feeling. In fact, I've probably seen you in a dream as I fly past you in the clouds, holding to the air like a wobbly bicycle rider.

Swisher Sweets

She was only doing her job. It was the second time we went in the pharmacy. She said, "Hello, welcome," the same way she did yesterday. I walked up and down some aisles by the time we got in line to pay. I was looking at the Swisher Sweets. Suddenly, she leaped over the counter. She grabbed the plastic bag someone left behind and ran out the door. When she came back, she stepped over the counter like a sheriff getting on a horse.

Saint Francis Bottled Water

Pour some on the ground. Enough to make a puddle. Soon the birds will fly down from the trees to land around you.

Monorails

In the future, every town has a monorail. As mayor, you order one from the catalog. Tracks on cement stilts grown like flowers. A view from the trees, a rush of windows, backyards with washlines full of waving clothes.

Every half hour the doors swing open magically. All you have to do is be there, ready to walk inside.

Another Ride

Every ride is designed to give you a different life.
When you leave the coaster tracks of Spaceship
Earth, you will join the milling, smiling crowds
floating around until you fall into another ride.

Blimps

Seeing the skywriter reminded me, I used to see those a lot growing up. Not only words, they made strange shapes, anything that would stick to the sky like soft lint. You could also see a loud slow airplane fly over with some slogan trailing behind it. And best of all were the nights you would hear a hum and you knew what it was. Ripe as a watermelon floating over the silhouette roofs and trees: a blimp.

Up close you can tell the treehouse is just an illusion, made from concrete and steel, with stairs that tick around from room to room. Back on the ground, you need a moment to check the flower to see if it's real.

A parking lot wide as a lake. There must be a thousand ordinary cars. What do I remember about ours?

Miss Susan Vaughn, Automaton

He knew who she was. He rented her shoes every night. They were red as Dorothy's slippers. Otherwise she bowled in drab 1940s clothes. Yes, it was obvious she was different. She moved mechanically while she rolled a perfect score every frame. She was amazing to watch. If she had gone missing from the amusement park, he wasn't going to tell.

The Flannel Alligator

Cold mornings don't bother this creature. Waiting for the sun, wearing plaid; I don't want to get close enough to see if it's wearing slippers.

Opening Joke for Ponce de Léon

"Can you believe I got here without a map?"

A Gorilla Clue

Tired of waiting for the elevator, I took the stairs. On the second landing, someone punched a hole in the wall. It might have been done by a gorilla.

Mop & Bucket

We don't have the language for conversation.
Only a couple awkward words held out like the
mop and bucket he carries.

The Spoonbill

Our first day in Florida, we drove past a spoonbill. It was standing in the runoff pool next to
the interstate. I still have a hard time believing
it was real.

When we return, the beds are made and more instant coffee has magically appeared. Imagine if you didn't know there were all these people working behind the scenes.

The Mermaid's Room

I stood in the cold Atlantic until my feet went numb and then the mermaid called me. She promised I'd be fine once I swam out past the breakers. The sea would comfort me. The water would hold me like the blankets covering her bed.

We heard it snowed again back home. A strange radio signal from another planet. We are surrounded here by sunlight and fantasy where people are spun until they're reeling.

The Squirrel

The squirrel doesn't like the cold morning pavement. When it stops, it holds a paw under its arm and stares at me with all the pity it can muster.

Snowbank on Wheels

Used to seeing winter, I think the parked white van is a snowbank.

The Russian Submarine

A garbage barge is dragged slowly out to sea.
Artifacts of Florida will sink like a shipwreck
and cover the ocean floor. It's turning into a
sliver on the horizon when someone behind us
asks the waitress if that's a Russian submarine.

Jerry Lewis

Jerry Lewis can't walk by a swimming pool without falling in.

I was a little surprised how easily she told him her secret, "I can fly."

Elvis Presley

When Elvis Presley felt this way, he would call you over to the screen door. Look out there. In the driveway is a brand new Cadillac he bought for you.

Orange Peels

Like the clothes we leave on the floor and the
chair.

Washed in the sink with a bar of hand soap. Left on the radiator. Poor things. They never expected this.

The Calliope Charms

The miners tumble like apples from the ground. Their lamps reflect rain across the bricks. Their picks click when they rest them to roll cigarettes. They leave their dust glimmering in puddles. I can't wait to tell you what I've seen, why I am late, why I'm so wet, and when I open my hand there's gold in it.

Glazed to rainbows, her smile belonged in a museum. She could warm you into a tremble, and leave you on your back in a shadow. The Girl with the Pottery Teeth was the city's one and only true beauty until I arrived: the Boy with the Light Bulb Ears.

This is not about me and my teeth. Oh, those ears! I can't wait to see him again. Before I go, I check my smile, brush my hair, one last look at myself in the mirror to make sure. My heart feels like the hum of a wishing wheel when I open the door.

Part 3
They Do Whatever It Is They Do

They spoke to each other in poetry rhymes.
Closer and closer. There were invisible forces at
play, oceans and forests and electricity in the air
as she leaned forward and with the gentleness
breathed onto flowers, she whispered in his ear.

She Spins the Round

Carnival eyes are all watching her spin without a net. Josephine is a tightrope walker, cloudy and dreamy on the wire, regardless of the drop. Her shadow paces underneath. It has to stay out of the lights as it rolls, ready to catch her if she falls, hiding between elephant feet.

The Cow on the Moon

She sings songs of loneliness with her harp-woven moo. She's jumped this far, now she doesn't know what to do.

Back to Ocean and Land

She sets her hooves on stars. To move home between so much outer space she takes her time,
stepping on each bright shine, until the blue
planet Earth becomes large enough to fall back
onto like a bedsheet of ocean and land.

A Chair for Manatees

As far as I know, it hasn't been done. Nobody has put a rocking chair underwater in the slow moving tide for that reason. The skids could make tracks in the buttery sand.

She looked at them all at The Talking Dog store. Finally, she settled on a poodle who spoke French. She also bought a bowl, a blanket, and records so she could learn the language.

Chocolate Hair

"Oh that chocolate hair!" cried the dentist in love with the girl in his chair.

You Are Made of Flowers

How did all these leaves and petals gather into all the right shapes and colors? When you lie yourself down, like a garden tended by the sun.

Ann Margaret

Ann Margaret is in love. That's not the sort of secret she can hide.

The Robot

The Robot has a list of errands to do. This hap-
pens every day. Life is not a program though.
He finally figured that out. It's a beautiful day.
Why miss a minute? Even a butterfly knows
that.

Would I miss the seasons if I lived where it was always sunny? Not really. But if I got nostalgic, I could call someone. Outside the post office, I would open a box of red leaves and feel the cold breath of what I left behind.

Plastic Telephone

When he was only two or so, our son had a plastic telephone toy. It would ring and he would talk to Mimiko in Japan. We never quite knew what they were saying.

On the corner of Forest Street and Champion was a shop that made rocking chairs. One glowed on a pedestal in the front window. They had dreams of making a living with the smooth sanded bones of a flying dinosaur.

Florida Lizard

They run just out of eye's reach. All you ever see
is a leaf shudder in the ivy.

A Wild Goose Chase

Who cares? The wooded path is warm today.
We've already gone three miles out of our way.

Guess what I did in 1944? I would stand in the field and watch the contrails and every once in a while a plane would fall.

Lobsters

Florida has a lot of aquariums. They grow on the walls like windows. The star of them all was the lobster tank. You could feel their eyes on you as you passed by on the way to your table.

The Wolf of Cocoa Beach

It took years for her to get that way, with the
sun knowing her like a lover.

Puppet arms flail for the "Satellite Blip Flip" and when he was done, not a sound from the audience…They didn't get it…So few did. He was real gone, as far out as the asteroid belt.

Bicycles

One night in college many moons ago, my friend and I raided the room where security would hide abandoned bicycles. The door was padlocked, but there was a gap above it and we could climb down inside. Bikes were piled on top of each other in there like ragged prisoners. They had given up hope ever seeing daylight again. We got as many as we could carry outside and stuck them in the trees over the campus walkway. The next day they were a source of wonder and the school paper even had a photo on the front page, baffled by who had done it and what it meant.

The Daily Fly

When I sit on the sunny bench I disturb a rest-
ing fly. I try to read the newspaper it left in
such a hurry, but I don't have a microscope.

Morris Teahorn

Actually that statue you see there in the park, heroically covered with pigeons, wearing the gray clothes and crooked hat from another century, isn't really a statue at all. His name is Morris Teahorn. He's been walking across the park for two hundred years. His progress has been tracked in paintings, a woodcut, postcard etchings and photography. As of today, he's halfway to where he thinks he should be.

Remember Abbott and Costello when the two of them stumbled through our room with a television set, rocking it in slow motion back and forth, tipping in the socket and turning the antenna towards Canada and beyond.

Excuses run to the horizon, promises he'll be here soon to nail the carpet ends down, replace shingles lost to the wind, but he has troubles everywhere he goes: a ghost haunts another rental house, his spine needs a new shark bone put in, the washer and dryer he brought us lacks a heating element…I had to turn it all off, collect everything he ever said into three garbage cans spray-painted Curly, Larry and Moe.

21 Circus Rooms

"Constructed by the Pullman Company in 1950, sold in 1970 to a circus, converted to 21 small rooms for the performers, it toured the country for 23 years."

"Egyptian Giant, The Living Skeleton, Double Bodied Wonder, Sword Swallower, Moss Haired Girl, Human Skye Terrier, What Is She?, Bearded Lady, Tattooed Man And Woman, East Indian Dwarf, Marvelous Pig, No Armed Wonder, Japanese Lady Magician, Armless Girl, India Rubber Man, Great Exhibitionist, Human Pin Cushion, The Georgia Magnet, Glass Eater, Human Calculator."

Eddie, pt. 1

Wouldn't you know I met him again while getting gas? This was years ago and he had a crumpled sort of car, but he's quieter than ever before. He asked me, "Don't I know you from somewhere?"

Eddie, pt.2

It was true—flash and I was there—tromping through the gravel pit searching for gold like pirates and later on fights and girls.

Eddie, pt.3

The playground terrors, words and whatevers,
when the school bus shook with Alice Cooper
and eggs thrown from the bridge. All so far
from where we are now.

A Florida Clown

Out in the parking lot it was night. Cars were always going by, their lamps yawned over his dark wall like searchlights or shooting stars.

The Ocelot

When he rented an apartment he told the landlord he had "a kitty." It was quiet and sleek and its spots had a lulling hypnotic power. The truth wasn't revealed until the cat marked its territory on the radiator vent. That violent smell drove all the other tenants outside at midnight onto the chopped lawn. They stared like moths as the ocelot came out and that was the end of its stay. To its way of thinking, the jungle was forever gone, its home of walls was always shifting; there was something very wrong with the world.

A. Robins, The Banana Man

He runs onto an empty stage in a huge black overcoat the size of a billowing garage. With the orchestra playing like a merry-go-round, he makes every sort of furniture unfold from his shadow. By the end of his act the entire stage is filled with things that weren't there before

A wooden stage with a movie screen built on the sand of that tropical island in World War 2. Soldiers watch the horizon for a steamship, or an airplane from the States flying low, beneath the enemy's radar.

A Starfish

She drifted with the rivers that floated through the alleys and pooled against the walls. The last time we saw her, she sat beside the bank fountain. We stopped to count the coins glittering like goldfish. 22. She reached in her deepest pocket and gave our daughter a starfish.

Dr. Biocal's Butterflies
Chapter 1:

Burrowed to new heights underground, Dr. Biocal's electric shadows roamed back and forth, feverish at work making deadly butterflies. Lording over the line of pinned, stainglass wings, his magnified eye looming like a hole in the moon, he attached a poisonous spine to each specimen. When the fleet was prepared, Dr. Biocal freed each butterfly into a cell imprisoned in the hollowed disguise of a violin case.

Chapter 2:

Out in the blue day, The Flower Society buzzed around the park gardens. Hidden in leaves, Dr. Biocal spied from a periscope holed in the ground. Their feet moved near and he could hear their purrs to orange begonias. Snaking like part of the roots, Dr. Biocal pushed the violin case through the brush and opened it. As it burst, he fell back underground to watch what happened next. What he saw was like a silent film panic, the cast falling and running into each other. He laughed at the view.

Chapter 3:

The movie didn't stay that way. Susan Fenton arrived and knew what to do, finding a sprinkler hose and spraying the danger away. Dr. Biocal snarled at the picture of it, but it wasn't quite over yet. Dark clouds formed overhead. The wet sound of clapping raindrops on leaves became a hundred angry butterflies returning in a waterfall down the tunnel to him.

First of all, let me say that I'm not. I'm sure I have other contenders. Just because I rose to the top and I live in a palace surrounded by a tall stone wall, cut off from the cries of the world. Who cares if I'm despised and hunted by roving helicopters and satellites? Like anyone else, I wake in the morning to the priceless singing of the birds.

The Cloud Driver

He would find a cloud, just the right size, and mold it into a car.

the
flying
machine
of
mr.
green

I EXPECT TO
FLY A HUNDRED
YARDS!

IGNITE THE FUSE!

BANG!

LOOK AT ME !!
I'M FLYING !

the

end

A Chair for Manatees: The Movie

Jessica Lange sits in a Laundromat. A full moon glows on the window. While the machines spin and Buddy Holly sings from a transistor, she looks over her shoulder, outside. A man standing in the bed of a pickup truck is throwing furniture into the sea.

The Talking Tiger

Last night everyone in this room dreamed of a talking tiger.

Broken Paddle

A shopping cart pushed by a mother with a broken leg. One kid is sitting in front of her, the others following behind. She moves her leg flat and straight out to the side and back and forth like an oar.

The Shoe Salesman

When I was little, you would sit on a wooden slanted footstool before a wall made of shoes and the shoe salesman would measure your feet, making small talk like everyone did at that time. Then he would go through a curtained doorway to return with a cardboard box. The shoe salesman was one of those old fashioned sorts of jobs like a 1950s gas station where your car was treated like a living creature.

Bookies

It was raining, only a little, and we were talking about the election next week. Everywhere there are signs and stickers and spots on TV buzzing this thing into everyone's attention. "Every election is rigged," the driver told me. "But if you want to know who's going to win, you have to ask a bookie." The bookies are choosing the president. They meet underneath the elevated train, their window rattles every time the wheels go by.

Our first moth hung around the house upside-down on the ceilings of rooms, following us throughout day and night. Using magic, it seemed to be in more than one place at a time. By and by we realized there was more than one. They liked to gather in the bathroom, wrap the shower curtain over their shoulders or hang on the wall like paintings.

Garage Sale Joke

"The lawnmower is free," the man said. He pointed from the porch. The rusted machine was left in the tall grass beside the sidewalk. A piece of string ran around it to hold some part of the engine on. "Does it work?" I said. "No," he explained, "That's why it's free."

The Gardenia

Yes, of course she's a knockout in her green caped uniform, but she sticks to her little yard where she tends growing vegetables and some flowers. "What about all the crime out there?" I ask her. We were sharing tea on the porch, the sun was climbing gently down the branches of the apple tree. She made a kind of flat tire sound and smiled, her hands tipped the way they talk in Italy.

7 Pictures

Janice Porch fell in love in 1942. It must have been the work of grinning angels, the heady draw of lobelia poised over everything. She got married in a week. Then the tall soldier was taken away. Seven pictures remained. She had to think hard of his face, even when she held the photographs. His body next to her always ended before his head, cropped off out of the frame. Funny at first and sad at last, each one like a sunflower with the top chopped off.

He was waiting in morning on the bleak ceiling next to the hot sun of the light bulb. 75 watts sizzled on his brown wings, contemplating.

Tourist Attraction

A San Francisco sailor eating spaghetti alone.

On break today I met the reading fly again.
This time I sat at the other end of the bench.
I listened for the sound of him turning pages.

Found by the reeds beside the road, an abandoned car, warm engine rattling, a baby sleeping on the seat.

Alexander Graham Bell carried his invention with him wherever he went. And he made a grand point of stopping on the boulevard every so often to talk into it. His loud words would trail off in crowds, into served meals getting cold; his laugh would bray as he carried on with his monologue. He seemed oblivious to the glances around him as if he was half mad, in contact with some other world.

He crumbles around the place like pecked suet.

Following Zorro to and fro all around Old Mexico, the alleys, walls and anywhere else in town he might leave a Z. I tracked that letter clue over the hills, into the next valley. They led to a railroad track and the last Z fell on a rock before the start of a suspension bridge. When the stone gave way a little, I could hear the subterranean gnashing of gears as a secret entrance woke up under the girders.

He pulled the curtain aside and the crowd screamed in horror. All the terror that could be expressed by human beings at seeing their worst fears. Then he closed the curtain. They had paid their dollars and there were more waiting in lines outside. They left shaking and holding each other for support.

I had to laugh at 2:23 AM when I heard the phone ringing next door and someone crashing in the dark like Bela Lugosi flagging a taxi.

Yor, the headless horror mutant from space's long distance: he foretells the future in the palm of his werewolf daughter.

Old What's-His-Face

He was in the 6th grade and already he was known to be a dog stabber. So when he told us he was going to jump off the moving school bus, we guessed he really would. The bus just happened to be passing my house when he bolted out the emergency door. I got out the usual way, past the driver talking on her radio. Walking up our driveway, I sensed him off in the forest like a panicked deer. Once the bus had rumbled away, I could hear him breaking through the brush. Even now you know just as much about him as I do.

Inspector Ozawa

Maker of the metal heart, he walks along the beach littered with shopping carts, watching the sea for spare parts

For an encore, he whirled the planet in the palm of his hand. He left it spinning recklessly on the beak of a crow and went out with a showgirl on each arm.

SHARK-CAGE

SMITH

"goes fishin'"

OKAY FELLAHS--
LOWER ME INTO
THE FRENZY

DOWN I GO!

WOW!
ROAR

SHARK-CAGE SMITH
IS LOWERED INTO
A FOUNTAIN

WHAT'S THE BIG
IDEA POPS?

TAKE ME BACK
UP!

the end

A Frog

The cashier has a frog in her throat. The day is ending at last. The sky is empty. She gets home and watches TV. Before she sleeps, she puts the frog in a china cup beside her bed.

Over Milkweed

The air is rare over milkweed. Things float or fly by (sounds, smells, shadows, temperature) dots of traveling pollen, bumblebees and butterflies. Swallows glide across in the hot afternoon. This land is its own little island. The whippoorwill still wakes up in the arching tree. This favorite place has not been traded away. It seems far out of reach, upwind and across a field, but something is happening too fast to stop. A cow on the other side of the old stone wall…another one too…then a little further off, where the ground is clawed, new houses have been built overnight. The way those houses are growing and spreading closer, it may not be long before the milkweed is plowed over too, changed into tar or concrete and turned into a memory. Under the tall tree, the milkweed meadow is only one more treasure in the way of something hungrier and bigger and always looking for more.

I spotted him in the lobby on that big marble floor full of chairs stuck in a holding pattern, surrounded by plastic plants. He wore green overalls with the name *Arbor Experts* sewn on the back. He hovered over each plant, choosing to examine a leaf or two on every fake tree. What was he doing? Why spend so much time on something only pretending to be alive?

Act 2:

I was curious. He was so good at his job, it wasn't until I crept quite near that I saw what was happening. Finding the right plastic leaf, he would decorate it with a plastic bug. Did it enhance the illusion that these plants were living things, attracting other living things? I suppose it did. There was a grasshopper on one leaf, a ladybug on another. A bee rested near a yellow soulless flower. An aphid so small he used tweezers. I wondered if he was paid to do this job. I wondered if this was only the start of my noticing there were other things like this going on around me.

Act 3:

As I lingered too long beside a pair of katydids, another man appeared next to me. "Excuse me," he said. He wore a pair of overalls too. They were blue. As I stepped aside I read the words on his back, *Pest Control.* With a brush, he swept the leaf I was concentrating on. His prey fell into a tin bucket he held with his other hand. He carried on, finding more. The sound of his progress was the ticking fade of plastic bugs filling that bucket.

A Duck

She wants to come back as a duck. If there's any chance when this life is over, if there are street signs to follow on the other side, or buttons to press; if there's any way she can possibly choose, that's what she wants. She's been practicing too—she can make a flawless quack. And it will be such a wonderful new life she insists, water and land will be her home and she can fly and best of all a duck never needs anything more than the world it is born into.

A Cat

There's a cat who lives on campus. I've seen her twice this week as I ride my creaking bicycle. Yesterday morning she ran sleek in front of me, chased by two crows into the tall garden leaves.

Snow White Moth

Holding the concrete wall, thoughts turned off, calm as snow.

You could actually leave Food Giant carrying a symphony. Besides the orchestra of tin cans, bags, bottles and bulk fruit and vegetables, for a few weeks they sold records of the Great Composers. A big cardboard display was positioned at the center aisle. That might have been my introduction to Beethoven and classical music, walking home, carrying a loaf of bread and a Mozart LP.

1: Going from zoo to zoo isn't easy to do. There's the snow in Cleveland, the hot big raindrops off the Gulf of Mexico, Montana hills, Wyoming wind, the crowded air of big cities, the roadside attractions where the heat waves shimmer off the tar. What would an animal have to do to be shuttled back and forth like this? I guess it's because I'm one of a kind. I'm sent in cars, the backs of trucks, pushed into boxcars. I don't know how many cages I've been in. Just once though, I'd like to get out. I know enough of the world from watching, I think I'd be okay out there.

2: I bet I could fit right in. A natural mimic, I've practiced their ways. Whenever nobody's around at night in the gloom, I walk with a cane, I hold a phone to my ear. All I have to do is wait for my chance. I know it will happen someday, I try not to lose faith although after 200 zoos, I feel a little unglued. If the door stays locked, if I can't get out then I have to keep hoping for the best. What else can I do? Pray? Okay. I hope to find myself in a cage that isn't a cage, a zoo that isn't a zoo, a perfect home for a tired old animal like me.

The Spectacular Failure of Gaston LeFlue, 1891

"Yes, yes," he told everyone. "I have seen the morning paper." Of course he had, it was hard to miss his face on the front page. His arm like a broken wing folded in front of him. "C'est la vie," he shrugged. After months of building his flying bird—crafting each feather to fit the wooden skeleton—moving it slowly by wagon through town to the bridge over the river, holding onto it, then leaping.

The Girl Who is the River

The girl who is the river would show up where we gathered to play hide and seek games in the park or throw a ball in the field. Sometimes when we were just walking along somewhere, she would be there. She might appear randomly at your yard, her brown hands on the fence, wearing soaking clothes muddy and torn at the edges. You never knew how long she would stay, if she would be daydreaming and slow, or would she only be with us for a minute and go?

Huckleberries

Going for a walk in the Chuckanut Hills, we discover true to its name it's mostly uphill. Looking for huckleberries, only found three or four. It's not their season yet. Everything calm and in place where it belonged, from the tops of the trees down the mossy bark to the ghost mushrooms and little yellow flowers. Searching as we hiked along, it was only the huckleberries I couldn't find. In all that green, I was thinking of jobs off through those leaves below the steep sides of fern and cedar and fir. It's a far way to where people rush around like ants. The other day I watched a crew laying tar. I was thinking about jobs. I'm looking for a better one. When it will arrive and where is not that different than me up here looking for huckleberries.

A Silent Movie

Each dawn this week a silent movie routine plays out as a man and a woman appear in the yard. They both wear black and gray and quietly reenact the scenes of the villain tying the girl to the railroad tracks. You can almost hear the sound of his wicked chuckling and her cries for help among the music of the morning bird routine.

New Shoes

They are displayed like shiny cars on tops of shelves and we're looking for something to carry him along a whole summer's worth of sunshine, beaches, airports, sidewalks, bicycle pedals, basketball courts and badminton grass. From concrete to forest, new shoes will be the next best thing to magic.

A Bat

Evening coming on, we stop when a bat ap-
pears, pedaling the air almost frantic to stay
aloft, with the last rays of sun stretched taut in
its wings

A Rabbit

Our dog stops still as she can get, hoping to match heartbeats with the animal she can't help bolting at.

I don't know how to tune a piano. Will I tell them though? If I fill out the application with all the right information and if I pass the interview and miraculously get the job, what will happen when I find myself sitting before a sick piano? Odd as the open hood of some exotic car, what will I do with my handful of delicate tools? Wondering what sort of music I could make from it, placing my hands on the keys, the wires and pedals, hoping like crazy that some cure will come to me.

"You will think nothing has happened, but after an hour you will get sleepy. That's from the neurotoxic poison…It will be hard to talk, things will blur. Your breathing will become difficult. You will lie down. Your heart will simply stop…Actually, it's not a bad way to go."

They're so good at hiding you wouldn't know coyotes are living in the trees across the street until 4 AM when the coal train rumbles through town. The horn sets off a coyote sobbing, giving them away.

Two Crows

Two crows atop the scaffold watching everyone
scurry.

That Flower

That flower calls out to be seen. Tipped just
right to catch light, I almost fall in.

Crows

Crows spilled out around a garbage can.

Blackberries

Carrying buckets on a green beach we stop when we reach the blackberry wave. It rises from the grass, breaking with a spray of thorns curling overhead. The ground is stained in little dots where berries have dropped. We each take our places along the hundred feet of vine pipelines looking for berries pumped up from some underground ocean splashing for miles in the dark. The sea down there must be so sweet we fill three buckets before we leave.

The look on your face is the reason I bought three.

Richard Is Gone

Richard is gone today, or so he says, off by bus. The Greyhound will make eleven stops, 36 hours on the road before he gets out onto that pebbled cement in that California air. It's different there. The sunlight is like a sort of golden paint and through all the traffic you can still smell the eucalyptus and the flowers and maybe even see orange and avocado trees. I sit here and think of it, and I can feel it. That's the power of the dream calling me.

The Reddish Dog

A hundred or so homeless are outside the window of the lodge. They form together to get food, but first they must listen while the mayor or someone tells them a lesson. I look away. On the ledge above the window are a bunch of Salish crows or maybe they're children, it's hard to tell. Some of them wear cedar masks. I speak to them in a crow imitation that comes out, "Hah." I have the sound right but there's no meaning to it. I don't seem to know that crow language has words hidden inside the sound. One of the children up there looks at the others and says, "Hah." I leave that place and cross a street running like a river to a parking lot on the other side. There's an opened-up abandoned car. Something is moving in a paper bag. At first it's a cat, but it becomes a reddish dog. It looks so hopeless and forgotten and hungry. I pet the sad-eyed dog and comfort it and tell it I'll be right back as I wake up.

The Dark Boat

I don't have to think of it. I can let it sail away from me. The tall walls are trapped with un-happy souls like the drops in a rain barrel that took years to fill.

My son grabs my hand—at the end of the aisle we see the local author, sharing the floor at the Dollar Store. Who knows what he's buying or what brings him here? He leaves the row with a vanilla soda and a bag of chips. When I catch another glimpse from a long distance I wonder, "Will what he's thinking about become another golden story? Should we feel lucky being this close to glory?" If we are, then why do we stay hiding around the corner?

The unnoticed bird sings from a tree, from a nest nobody can see. The story isn't lost. We all know how it goes.

Two cherry trees hover over the tall wooden fence. A dog is barking.

Really And Truly

My grandmother used that expression a lot. She was checking her flowers on the roadside the morning she met the garbage man. "Thank you," she told him. He couldn't believe she said that. She told me, "Really and truly. I wish I had a camera to catch his face."

The Old Astronaut

Step by step, one breath leading to another, he follows the sidewalk.

The Sleepy Tiger

Sunlight made the tiger sleepy on the lawn. It lay down by the remains of its last meal, in no rush to eat again.

Territory

The road through this flat green dream. I'm not looking for gold or territory. We're thirty minutes from Orlando, with half a tank of gas.

Cape Canaveral

Once upon a time, there was a direct connection between the moon and Florida.

This is My Bread and Butter

Sitting on a lawn chair in the sun. Of course I got something done! I've been working on this book, haven't I?

Beethoven Sonata #8 Performed by a Snowman

By the end, all that's left is a violin in a pool of water.

A Dead Honey Bee

She didn't work there long but I liked her.
I knew she liked movies and we were talking
about Hemingway's *To Have and Have Not* and
that bee we never got to see.

The Palm Reader

I don't know what to say to a palm tree. They're strange to me. I would need to be here more than three days to get used to them, to understand a language that grows tall as a giraffe.

Florida Crickets

We left you that night with crickets surround-
ing our rental car.

Spirit Airlines

The last morning in Florida, in a hotel room we'll never see again. We're like everyone else; we come and we go.

A Bird

Once the plane is steady, high up in the slip-stream at cruising altitude, I open my eyes and notice the stewardess has turned into a bird. Her body sparkled with blue and violet feathers and her long neck bent down like sloping ballet. Then, as she raised her wings, we all fell back asleep again.

Flying Tangerine

18,000 feet above Texas, a Japanese grandmother eats a tangerine.

Heaven

Everyone asks what it was like. The light, the flowers, the warmth. How could anyone forget Heaven? Who wouldn't want to go back? It's still happening while we're not there, supposing we will return.

A big formation of swans overhead. The early sun sparks on their hinges.

Winter Flowers

The snow that covered the field has turned into daisies and someone on the shore is feeding the ducks, drawing them near with torn bits of Wonder Bread.

The Mallards

Radio-controlled by spring to arrive every year
and float like wooden shoes on the shallow
pond.

Singing Sunlight

The birds of the woods are singing sunlight on
trees that are still tightly holding in their leaves.

Park Avenue Records on a rainy night. I watched her move behind the counter, sweater like a bee, as she put another album on. Music and golden light. I wasn't the only one who worshiped her. We went in and out the door.

Nostalgia City

Abandoned lots and Five & Dimes, climbing trees and the places we used to be. If you live somewhere long enough, you see things come and go. It's the lesson you don't want to know, that life is teaching you all the time. There's no such thing as forever, it's gone right before your eyes.

ICU2TV

A clown looks out from a hollow TV, across
Queen Anne Hill, Phinney Ridge, Green Lake,
Rainier Valley and all the neighborhoods in be-
tween. A spiral wheel is painted on his door.
When it spins, it opens to a cartoon world.

The Start of Japan

The first cherry tree has bloomed on 32nd Street. That sounds like the start of Japan. There goes another one. The bus window is a movie screen.

The Daffodil Gang

On the street corner, a gang of daffodils loiter,
looking at the ground when I walk by.

Apples

Build a fantasyland where you are. Believe it or
not, it doesn't take much. After work I carried
a round stone home and put it by the bowl of
apples.

Who knows exactly when it happened but you can see the footprints that went across that cement when it was fresh and wet.

A Reversed Man

On a Frankenstein night in 1938, Dr. Biocal wired a cat to rows of lights and switches and pulled the lever. A lightning bolt hit, lit the steep city rooftops. The world's first reversed cat snapped free of the tangled burning wires and jumped out the window. Dr. Biocal stood on the fire escape landing, held onto the metal railing, searching the dark. Below him, the sidewalk rattled with a big maple leaf. The streetlamp gave it a black cat-sized shadow. Days passed. He never saw it again. A week later, he tried the experiment on himself. Maybe he's out there now, A Reversed Man, walking the streets; the wrong side of the road looks right.

The World is Cliff Link

Today, the world is Cliff Link who woke up sad
and confused.

Cliff Link Makes a Telephone Call

On the way somewhere, he stopped and fed a telephone booth. He had a feeling she would answer and when she did he didn't know what to say.

Nobody else on the bus this morning. I walk down the empty aisle and announce to the driver with a flourish, "Take me to the Opera House!"

A 1973 Dream

Two weeks after Florida, I went back in a dream. We pull up in a van and the 1970s cop show soundtrack lets us know something is happening. The mob is involved. Everyone is wearing suits. We trick the guard into thinking the plane is delayed. Once he leaves, we switch tickets and send her instead. She wears big round sunglasses and a disguise.

A 1944 Movie

With a starring role as a hardboiled gangster in
my dream, we have time to share a cigarette.
I watch the smoke. I laugh at what happened
this life, at the years that took us apart.

He brought a stack of papers for us to sign. After half an hour of that routine, he took our documents and put them in his suitcase. He held the table to stand up. He used a cane to limp outside. He explained away some disaster that occurred long ago. When he got in his car, that was it, he was off to another appointment.

I introduce myself to the people who live in the apartment next door. I pet their cat when it runs up to me. Then all of a sudden I vanish. I wonder what they thought when that happened and their lives continued in that dream without me.

5 AM

I wake up and listen for that first bird. It always starts somewhere in the distance, somewhere closer to the rising sun.

It's still dark as night when I hear the first report. The birds in our yard are waiting for that news too. Passed along from wing to wing, across the country with the traveling light.

Now the tree outside our window is singing like a radio tower. I hear about the mountains, the plains, rivers, lakes, the cities and towns a hundred miles away. As I tune through their stations, I listen for that one little wren who tells me about Florida where another new day has already begun.

FLORIDA

Written by Allen Frost
mostly in March and April 2019

Books by Good Deed Rain

Saint Lemonade, Allen Frost, 2014. Two novels illustrated by the author in the manner of the old Big Little Books.

Playground, Allen Frost, 2014. Poems collected from seven years of chapbooks.

Roosevelt, Allen Frost, 2015. A Pacific Northwest novel set in July, 1942, when a boy and a girl search for a missing elephant. Illustrated throughout by Fred Sodt.

5 Novels, Allen Frost, 2015. Novels written over five years, featuring circus giants, clockwork animals, detectives and time-travelers.

The Sylvan Moore Show, Allen Frost, 2015. A short story omnibus of 193 stories written over 30 years.

Town in a Cloud, Allen Frost, 2015. A 3-part book of poetry, written during the Bellingham rainy seasons of fall, winter, and spring.

A Flutter of Birds Passing Through Heaven: A Tribute to Robert Sund, 2016. Edited by Allen Frost and Paul Piper. The story of a legendary Ish River poet & artist.

At the Edge of America, Allen Frost, 2016. Two novels in one book blend time travel in a mythical poetic America.

Lake Erie Submarine, Allen Frost, 2016. Two weeks in Ohio inspired these poems, illustrated by the author.

and Light, Paul Piper, 2016. Poetry written over three years. Illustrated with watercolors by Penny Piper.

The Book of Ticks, Allen Frost, 2017. A giant collection of 8 mysterious adventures featuring Phil Ticks. Illustrated throughout by Aaron Gunderson.

I Can Only Imagine, Allen Frost, 2017. Five adventures of love and heartbreak dreamed in an imaginary world. Cover & color illustrations by Annabelle Barrett.

The Orphanage of Abandoned Teenagers, Allen Frost, 2017. A fictional guide for teens and their parents. Illustrated by the author.

In the Valley of Mystic Light: An Oral History of the Skagit Valley Arts Scene, 2017. Edited by Claire Swedberg & Rita Hupy.

Different Planet, Allen Frost, 2017. Four science fiction adventures: reincarnation, robots, talking animals, outer space and clones. Cover & illustrations by Laura Vasyutynska.

Go with the Flow: A Tribute to Clyde Sanborn, 2018. Edited by Allen Frost. The life and art of a timeless river poet.

Homeless Sutra, Allen Frost, 2018. Four stories: Sylvan Moore, a flying monk, a water salesman, and a guardian rabbit.

The Lake Walker, Allen Frost 2018. A little novel set in black and white like one of those old European movies about death and life.

A Hundred Dreams Ago, Allen Frost, 2018. A winter book of poetry and prose. Illustrated by Aaron Gunderson.

Almost Animals, Allen Frost, 2018. A collection of linked stories, thinking about what makes us animals.

The Robotic Age, Allen Frost, 2018. A vaudeville magician and his robot track down ghosts. Illustrated throughout by Aaron Gunderson.

Kennedy, Allen Frost, 2018. This sequel to *Roosevelt* is a coming-of-age fable set during two weeks in 1962 in a mythical Kennedy-land. Illustrated throughout by Fred Sodt.

Fable, Allen Frost, 2018. There's something going on in this country and I can best relate it in fable: the parable of the rabbits, a bedtime story, and the diary of our trip to Ohio.

Elbows & Knees: Essays & Plays, Allen Frost, 2018. A thrilling collection of writing about some of my favorite subjects, from B-movies to Brautigan.

The Last Paper Stars, Allen Frost 2019. A trip back in time to the 20 year old mind of Frankenstein, and two other worlds of the future.

Walt Amherst is Awake, Allen Frost, 2019. The dreamlife of an office worker. Illustrated throughout by Aaron Gunderson.

When You Smile You Let in Light, Allen Frost, 2019. An atomic love story in NYC.

Pinocchio in America, Allen Frost, 2019. After 82 years buried underground, Pinocchio is resurrected in America.

Taking Her Sides on Immortality, Robert Huff, 2019. The long awaited poetry collection from a local, nationally renowned master of words.

Florida, Allen Frost, 2019. 3 days in Florida turned into a book of sunshine inspired stories.

spirit
airlines

BOARDING PASS

Customer Name
FROST/ALLEN

From
ORLANDO

To
LAS VEGAS

Gate	Boarding
34	**7:1!**
SUBJECT TO CHANGE	****NO CAR**

DOORS CLOSE 15 MINUTES BEFORE DEPARTURE

* 9 7 8 1 6 4 5 1 6 9 8 6 4 *